MIND YOUR MANNERS, B.B. WOLF

BY JUDY SIERRA

ILLUSTRATED BY J. OTTO SEIBOLD

MAIN Villa

SENIOR CENTER

OFFICE

Alfred A. Knopf · New York

For Alden Strup, with love and kisses
—J.S.

love forever, always, theadora, amelia, and ulysses
—J.O.S.

THIS IS A BORZOI BOOK PUBLISHED BY ALFRED A. KNOPF

Text copyright © 2007 by Judy Sierra • Illustrations copyright © 2007 by J. Otto Seibold

Published in the United States by Alfred A. Knopf, an imprint of Random House Children's Books, a division of Random House, Inc., New York.

KNOPF, BORZOI BOOKS, and the colophon are registered trademarks of Random House, Inc.

www.randomhouse.com/kids

Educators and librarians, for a variety of teaching tools, visit us at www.randomhouse.com/teachers

Library of Congress Cataloging-in-Publication Data
Sierra, Judy.
Mind your manners, B.B. Wolf / by Judy Sierra ; illustrated by J. Otto Seibold.
p. cm.
SUMMARY: When B.B. Wolf, who now lives in the Villain Villa Retirement Residence, is invited to the library for a storybook tea,
he is careful to follow the advice of his crocodile friend and impresses everyone with how polite he can be.
ISBN 978-0-375-83532-2 (trade) — ISBN 978-0-375-93532-9 (lib. bdg.)
[1. Etiquette—Fiction. 2. Characters in literature—Fiction. 3. Libraries—Fiction. 4. Humorous stories.] I. Seibold, J. Otto, ill. II. Title.
PZ7.S5773Min 2007   [E]—dc22   2006023951

The illustrations in this book were created using Adobe Illustrator.

MANUFACTURED IN CHINA • August 2007 • 10 9 8 7 6 5 4 3 2 1 • First Edition

One morning, B.B. Wolf huffed and puffed up the hill to his mailbox.

"Bills, bills, bills," he growled.

And something else.
What was in the mysterious envelope?

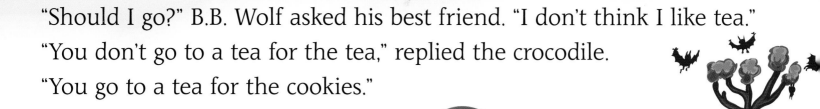

"Should I go?" B.B. Wolf asked his best friend. "I don't think I like tea."
"You don't go to a tea for the tea," replied the crocodile.
"You go to a tea for the cookies."

DO NOT
PICK THE FLOWERS

"Cookies," murmured B.B. Wolf longingly.

"You'll have to behave yourself," the crocodile warned.

B.B. Wolf chewed the end of his tail nervously. His friend consulted an etiquette book.

"Sip your tea, don't slurp," the crocodile read. "If you burp, say 'Excuse me.'"

B.B. Wolf made up a song to help himself remember.

On Tuesday afternoon, B.B. Wolf put on his best jacket.
"How do I look?" he asked.
"Dashing," declared the croc. "Now smile, have a good time, and don't bite anyone."

B.B. Wolf loped along the sidewalk, twirling his cane and singing,

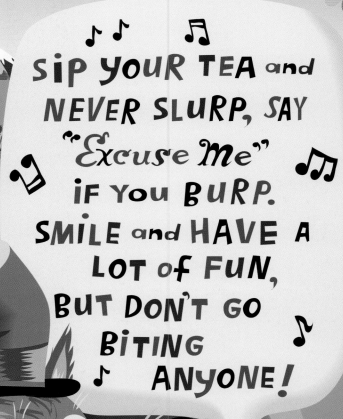

B.B. Wolf took a deep breath and opened the library door. Everyone turned to look at him. He smiled nervously.

"What a big smile you have!" exclaimed a girl in a red cape.

"The better to *greet* you with, my dear," B.B. Wolf replied.

GULP!

B.B. Wolf was beginning to have fun.
"How do you do, Mr. Wolf?" said a tall
woman. "I am Miss Wonderly, the librarian.
Would you like some tea?"

"Yes, please," said B.B. Wolf,
looking around for cookies.

Miss Wonderly poured a cup of tea.
Carefully, B.B. Wolf lifted the cup to his lips. Did he slurp?
No, he sipped slowly and quietly, still looking around for cookies.

After his third cup of tea, B.B. Wolf's tummy
felt funny and made a noise, *gurgle, gurgle*.
Bad luck! He'd forgotten what to say if he burped.
B.B. Wolf bent over the library computer. E-T-I-Q-U-E-T-T-E, he
typed, then hurried to the right shelf. He grabbed a book and
pawed through the pages, looking for the magic words.

HUMAN BEHAVIOR

ETIQUETTE

CLICKITY CLICK

GURGLE

GURGLE GURGLE

THE Etiquette BOOK

THE ETIQUETTE BOOK

THE Etiquette BOOK

Books bounced. Windows rattled. Walls shook.

"Run, run, as fast as you can!" screamed the
Gingerbread Boy.

"Run right back here!" called Miss Wonderly.

"B.B. Wolf!" giggled the Three Little Pigs. "You almost blew down the library." "What good *manners* you have!" exclaimed Miss Wonderly. "Most people don't say 'Excuse me' until *after* they burp."

B.B. Wolf smiled from ear to ear. "Let the good times roll!" he crooned. He strolled around the library and talked to everyone. "Looking good, Gingerbread Boy!" B.B. Wolf slapped the little guy on the back. "Did anyone ever tell you that you smell delicious . . . just like a cookie?"

"Cookie?" asked Miss Wonderly. She held out a tray of tiny gingerbread people.

"Dear me, no!" gasped B.B. Wolf. "I could never bite a cute little Gingerbread Boy."

"Mr. Wolf!" exclaimed Miss Wonderly. "You are so kind and sensitive. Storybooks don't do you justice."

At five o'clock, Miss Wonderly slipped a paper bag into B.B. Wolf's paws. "Enjoy these later," she said. "And thank you for coming to the library. The children love reading about you."

"You're welcome," said B.B. Wolf. "I'll drop by one day and tell you how these stories *really* happened."

A happy old wolf loped home, munching cookies as he sang,

EVEN IN A HOUSE of BRICKS, BIG BAD WOLVES CAN LEARN NEW TRICKS.

SIP your TEA and NEVER SLURP, SAY "EXCUSE ME" IF YOU BURP.

SMILE AND HAVE A LOT of FUN, BUT DON'T GO BITING ANYONE!

the End